IN REMEMBRANCE OF
"SAMMY",
THE INTELLIGENT PINK-EYED REPRESENTATIVE
OF A PERSECUTED (BUT IRREPRESSIBLE) RACE
AN AFFECTIONATE LITTLE FRIEND
AND MOST ACCOMPLISHED THIEF

FREDERICK WARNE

Published by the Penguin Group
Registered office: 80 Strand, London, WC2R ORL
Penguin Young Readers Group, 345 Hudson Street, New York, N.Y. 10014, USA

First published 1908 by Frederick Warne
This edition with new reproductions of Beatrix Potter's book illustrations first published 2007
This edition copyright © Frederick Warne & Co. 2007
New reproductions of Beatrix Potter's book illustrations copyright © Frederick Warne & Co. 2002
Original copyright in text and illustrations © Frederick Warne & Co., 1908

Frederick Warne & Co. is the owner of all rights, copyrights and trademarks
in the Beatrix Potter character names and illustrations.

Manufactured in China

THE TALE OF
SAMUEL WHISKERS
OR THE ROLY-POLY PUDDING
BY BEATRIX POTTER

FREDERICK WARNE

ONCE upon a time there was an old cat, called
Mrs. Tabitha Twitchit, who was an anxious parent.
She used to lose her kittens continually, and
whenever they were lost they were always
in mischief!

On baking day she determined to shut them up in
a cupboard.

She caught
Moppet and
Mittens, but she
could not find Tom.

Mrs. Tabitha
went up and
down all over the
house, mewing for

Tom Kitten. She looked in the pantry under the
staircase, and she searched the best spare bedroom
that was all covered up with dust sheets. She went
right upstairs and looked into the attics, but she
could not find him anywhere.

IT was an old, old house, full of cupboards and passages. Some of the walls were four feet thick, and there used to be queer noises inside them, as if there might be a little secret staircase. Certainly there were odd little jagged doorways in the wainscot, and things disappeared at night — especially cheese and bacon.

Mrs. Tabitha became more and more distracted, and mewed dreadfully.

WHILE their
mother was
searching the
house, Moppet
and Mittens had
got into mischief.

The cupboard door was not locked, so they pushed it open and came out.

They went straight to the dough which was set to rise in a pan before the fire.

They patted it with their little soft paws — "Shall we make dear little muffins?" said Mittens to Moppet.

BUT just at that moment somebody
knocked at the front door, and Moppet
jumped into the flour barrel in a fright.

Mittens ran away to the dairy,
and hid in an empty jar on the
stone shelf
where the milk
pans stand.

9

THE visitor was a neighbour, Mrs. Ribby; she had called to borrow some yeast.

Mrs. Tabitha came downstairs mewing dreadfully — "Come in, Cousin Ribby, come in, and sit ye down! I'm in sad trouble, Cousin Ribby," said Tabitha, shedding tears. "I've lost my dear son Thomas; I'm afraid the rats have got him." She wiped her eyes with her apron.

"He's a bad kitten, Cousin Tabitha; he made a cat's cradle of my best bonnet last time I came to tea. Where have you looked for him?"

"All over the house! The rats are too many for me. What a thing it is to have an unruly family!" said Mrs. Tabitha Twitchit.

"I'M not afraid of rats; I will help you to find
him; and whip him too! What is all that soot in
the fender?"

"THE chimney wants sweeping — Oh, dear me,
Cousin Ribby — now Moppet and Mittens are
gone!

"They have both got out of the cupboard!"

RIBBY and Tabitha set to work to search the house thoroughly again. They poked under the beds with Ribby's umbrella, and they rummaged in cupboards. They even fetched a candle, and looked inside a clothes chest in one of the attics. They could not find anything, but once they heard a door bang and somebody scuttered downstairs.

"Yes, it is infested with rats," said Tabitha tearfully. "I caught seven young ones out of one hole in the back kitchen, and we had them for dinner last Saturday. And once I saw the old father rat — an enormous old rat, Cousin Ribby. I was just going to jump upon him, when he showed his yellow teeth at me and whisked down the hole.

"The rats get upon my nerves, Cousin Ribby," said Tabitha.

14

RIBBY and Tabitha searched and searched.
They both heard a curious roly-poly noise under
the attic floor. But there was nothing to be seen.

They returned to the kitchen. "Here's one of your
kittens at least," said Ribby, dragging Moppet out
of the flour barrel.

They shook the
flour off her and
set her down on
the kitchen floor.
She seemed to be
in a terrible fright.

"OH! Mother, Mother," said Moppet,
"there's been an old woman rat in the kitchen,
and she's stolen some of the dough!"

The two cats ran to look at the dough pan.
Sure enough there were marks of little scratching
fingers, and a lump of dough was gone!

"Which way did she go, Moppet?"

But Moppet had been too much frightened
to peep out of the barrel again.

Ribby and Tabitha took her with them to keep

her safely in
sight, while
they went on
with their
search.

17

THEY went into the dairy.

The first thing they found was Mittens, hiding in an empty jar.

They tipped up the jar, and she scrambled out.

"Oh, Mother, Mother!" said Mittens —

"Oh! Mother, Mother, there has been an old man rat in the dairy — a dreadful 'normous big

rat, Mother; and he's stolen a pat of butter and the rolling-pin."

Ribby and Tabitha looked at one another.

"A rolling-pin and butter! Oh, my poor son Thomas!" exclaimed Tabitha, wringing her paws.

"A rolling-pin?" said Ribby. "Did we not hear a roly-poly noise in the attic when we were looking into that chest?"

Ribby and Tabitha rushed upstairs again. Sure enough the roly-poly noise was still going on quite distinctly under the attic floor.

"This is serious, Cousin Tabitha," said Ribby. "We must send for John Joiner at once, with a saw."

NOW this is what had been happening to Tom Kitten, and it shows how very unwise it is to go up a chimney in a very old house, where a person does not know his way, and where there are enormous rats.

Tom Kitten did not want to be shut up in a cupboard. When he saw that his mother was going to bake, he determined to hide.

He looked about for a nice convenient place, and he fixed upon the chimney.

The fire had only just been lighted, and it was not hot; but there was a white choky smoke from the green sticks. Tom Kitten got upon the fender and looked up. It was a big old-fashioned fire-place.

THE chimney itself was wide enough inside for a man to stand up and walk about. So there was plenty of room for a little Tom Cat.

HE jumped right up into the fire-place, balancing himself upon the iron bar where the kettle hangs.

TOM KITTEN took another big jump off the bar, and landed on a ledge high up inside the chimney, knocking down some soot into the fender.

TOM KITTEN coughed and choked with the smoke; and he could hear the sticks beginning to crackle and burn in the fire-place down below. He made up his mind to climb right to the top, and get out on the slates, and try to catch sparrows.

"I cannot go back. If I slipped I might fall in the fire and singe my beautiful tail and my little blue jacket."

The chimney was a very big old-fashioned one. It was built in the days when people burnt logs of wood upon the hearth.

The chimney stack stood up above the roof like a little stone tower, and the daylight shone down from the top, under the slanting slates that kept out the rain.

TOM KITTEN
was getting
very frightened!
He climbed up,
and up, and up.
Then he waded
sideways through
inches of soot. He was like a little sweep himself.

It was most confusing in the dark. One flue
seemed to lead into another. There was less smoke,
but Tom Kitten felt quite lost. He scrambled up
and up; but before he reached the chimney top he
came to a place where somebody had loosened a

stone in the
wall. There
were some
mutton bones
lying about –

"THIS seems funny," said Tom Kitten. "Who has been gnawing bones up here in the chimney? I wish I had never come! And what a funny smell? It is something like mouse; only dreadfully strong. It makes me sneeze," said Tom Kitten.

HE squeezed through the hole in the wall, and dragged himself along a most uncomfortably tight passage where there was scarcely any light.

HE groped his way carefully for several yards; he was at the back of the skirting-board in the attic, where there is a little mark * in the picture.

ALL at once he fell head over heels in the dark, down a hole, and landed on a heap of very dirty rags.

When Tom Kitten picked himself up and looked about him — he found himself in a place that he had never seen before, although he had lived all his life in the house.

It was a very small stuffy fusty room, with boards, and rafters, and cobwebs, and lath and plaster.

Opposite to him — as far away as he could sit — was an enormous rat.

"What do you mean by tumbling into my bed all covered with smuts?" said the rat, chattering his teeth.

"PLEASE, sir, the chimney wants sweeping,"
said poor Tom Kitten.

"ANNA MARIA! Anna Maria!" squeaked the
rat. There was a pattering noise and an old woman
rat poked her head round a rafter.

ALL in a minute she rushed upon Tom Kitten, and before he knew what was happening —

His coat was pulled off, and he was rolled up in a bundle, and tied with string in very hard knots.

Anna Maria did the tying. The old rat watched her and took snuff. When she had finished, they both sat staring at him with their mouths open.

"Anna Maria," said the old man rat (whose name was Samuel Whiskers) — "Anna Maria, make me a kitten dumpling roly-poly pudding for my dinner."

"It requires dough and a pat of butter, and a rolling-pin," said Anna Maria, considering Tom Kitten with her head on one side.

"NO," said Samuel Whiskers, "make it properly, Anna Maria, with breadcrumbs."

"Nonsense! Butter and dough," replied Anna Maria.

The two rats consulted together for a few minutes and then went away.

Samuel Whiskers got through a hole in the wainscot, and went boldly down the front staircase to the dairy to get the butter. He did not meet anybody.

HE made a second journey for the rolling-pin. He pushed it in front of him with his paws, like a brewer's man trundling a barrel.

He could hear Ribby and Tabitha talking, but they were busy lighting the candle to look into the chest.

They did not see him.

ANNA MARIA went down by way of the
skirting-board and a window shutter to the
kitchen to steal the dough.

SHE borrowed a small saucer, and scooped
up the dough with her paws.

She did not observe Moppet.

WHILE Tom Kitten was left alone under the floor of the attic, he wriggled about and tried to mew for help.

But his mouth was full of soot and cobwebs, and he was tied up in such very tight knots, he could not make anybody hear him.

Except a spider who came out of a crack in the ceiling and examined the knots critically, from a safe distance.

It was a judge of knots because it had a habit of tying up unfortunate blue-bottles. It did not offer to assist him.

Tom Kitten wriggled and squirmed until he was quite exhausted.

PRESENTLY the rats came back and set to work to make him into a dumpling. First they smeared him with butter, and then they rolled him in the dough.

"Will not the string be very indigestible, Anna Maria?" inquired Samuel Whiskers.

ANNA MARIA said she thought that it was of
no consequence; but she wished that Tom Kitten
would hold his head still, as it disarranged
the pastry. She laid hold of his ears.

TOM KITTEN bit and spat, and mewed and wriggled; and the rolling-pin went roly-poly, roly; roly, poly, roly. The rats each held an end.

"His tail is sticking out! You did not fetch enough dough, Anna Maria."

"I fetched as much as I could carry," replied Anna Maria.

"I do not think" — said Samuel Whiskers, pausing to take a look at Tom Kitten — "I do *not* think it will be a good pudding. It smells sooty."

Anna Maria was about to argue the point when all at once there began to be other sounds up above — the rasping noise of a saw; and the noise of a little dog, scratching and yelping!

THE rats dropped the rolling-pin, and listened attentively.

"We are discovered and interrupted, Anna Maria; let us collect our property — and other people's — and depart at once.

"I fear that we shall be obliged to leave this pudding.

"BUT I am persuaded that the knots would
have proved indigestible, whatever you may
urge to the contrary."

"Come away at once and help me to tie up some
mutton bones in a counterpane," said Anna Maria.
"I have got half a smoked ham hidden in
the chimney."

SO it happened that by the time John Joiner had got the plank up — there was nobody under the floor except the rolling-pin and Tom Kitten in a very dirty dumpling!

BUT there was a strong smell of rats; and John
Joiner spent the rest of the morning sniffing and
whining, and wagging his tail, and going round
and round with his head in the hole like a gimlet.

THEN he nailed the plank down again, and put his tools in his bag, and came downstairs.

The cat family had quite recovered. They invited him to stay to dinner.

The dumpling had been peeled off Tom Kitten, and made separately into a bag pudding, with currants in it to hide the smuts.

They had been obliged to put Tom Kitten into a hot bath to get the butter off.

John Joiner smelt the pudding; but he regretted that he had not time to stay to dinner, because he had just finished making a wheelbarrow for Miss Potter, and she had ordered two hen-coops.

AND when I was going to the post late in the afternoon — I looked up the lane from the corner, and I saw Mr. Samuel Whiskers and his wife on the run, with big bundles on a little wheelbarrow, which looked very like mine.

They were just turning in at the gate to the barn of Farmer Potatoes.

Samuel Whiskers was puffing and out of breath. Anna Maria was still arguing in shrill tones.

She seemed to know her way, and she seemed to have a quantity of luggage.

I am sure *I* never gave her leave to borrow my wheelbarrow!

THEY went into the barn, and hauled their parcels with a bit of string to the top of the hay mow.

AFTER that, there were no more rats for
a long time at Tabitha Twitchit's.

AS for Farmer Potatoes, he has been driven nearly distracted. There are rats, and rats, and rats in his barn! They eat up the chicken food, and steal the oats and bran, and make holes in the meal bags.

And they are all descended from Mr. and Mrs. Samuel Whiskers — children and grand-children and great great grand-children.

There is no end to them!

MOPPET and Mittens have grown up into very good rat-catchers.

They go out rat-catching in the village, and they find plenty of employment. They charge so much a dozen, and earn their living very comfortably.

THEY hang up the rats' tails in a row on the barn door, to show how many they have caught — dozens and dozens of them.

BUT Tom Kitten has always been afraid of a rat;
he never durst face anything that is bigger than —

A Mouse.